THE JUNK DRAWER

A Place for our Dreams

RICKEY ALAN SMITH

ARPress
45 Dan Road Suite 15
Canton MA 02021
Hotline: 1(888) 821-0229
Fax: 1(508) 545-7580

Ordering Information:
Quantity sales. Special discounts are available on quantity purchases by corporations, associations, and others. For details, contact the publisher at the address above.

Printed in the United States of America.

ISBN-13:   Softcover   979-8-89676-412-0
                eBook   979-8-89676-413-7

Library of Congress Control Number: 2025909188

Marci, Kim, Dakota, and Janay are laughing and having a good time as they walk each other what we call down South as "piece a way home." Those who live the closest walk part of the way home with the person who lives the farthest. It was a time to reminisce the day's activities and say their last goodbye's until the next day. Kim stops suddenly and points toward The Thomas Street Liquor Store. It was a land mark for the area. Many businesses had come and gone including other liquor stores but Thomas Street Liquor managed to survive the times. The owner was an old Italian man named Joey. Joey looked to be 100 years old but he never seemed to have any physical problems. Joey had been in the neighborhood so long until he felt like he was an honorary resident and he was often treated as such. Some of the guys in the neighborhood would come by when it was near closing time and hang out to be sure nothing happened to him. But on this night something was radically wrong. Several young black men were yelling and throwing bricks and whatever they could find. The windows were knocked out and a small fire was burning in front of the store. Joey is standing outside pleading with the mob but he is ignored. No one attempts to hurt Joey but they were destroying his business. At this point none of the rioters were angry enough to hurt Joey but the same could not be said for an unfortunate white man who happens to be in the wrong place at the wrong time. Once he is spotted they rush over and begin kicking and hitting him. He is knocked to the ground and one of the men take his wallet. The man lies still and the mob walks away. The sounds of sirens probably saved his life. Joey goes over to help him along with some of the neighbors who were observing from their windows. Joey ponders why is it that innocent people suffer so? Although he understood their pain and anger caused by such a great loss he could think of no reason for such senseless acts of violence. Joey walks back to his store as the rioters continue to throw whatever they could find through his window. Some of the men were about to go into the store and loot but Boo Boo and John Reed walked up. There were approximately ten rioters but none of them wanted to try Boo Boo or John Reed. They both had reputations that they didn't mind backing up. Boo Boo reprimands them," You know this ain't right. Joey is a good dude." The rioters begin to walk away partly out of shame and partly out of fear of Boo Boo and John Reed.

Marci and her friends are terrified at what is unfolding before them. Kim screams,' Why are they doing this, what's happening." The sirens in the distance get louder and soon they witness police coming from every direction. The young men scatter including Boo Boo and John Reed. They know the police don't ask questions in situations like this. Some run through a nearby alley, others jump the fence behind the store and a few run to Flop's Pool Hall. No one really know how he got the name Flop but rumors say it was because of the way he dresses. He is only 4' 11" tall and his clothes hang off of his overweight body like a tarp. He was respected and some even think him to be pretty well off. The police exit the cars with shotguns drawn and shouting obscenities. "Stop, bring your black ass back here." The girls are frozen in place by what they are witnessing. Another policeman yells." Lets thump a few of these niggers" as they run into the pool hall in pursuit of those who ran in. When they enter everyone is playing pool as if nothing is happening. The police are familiar with Flop because the pool room has been around for years. They walk over to him and one policeman asks, "Where the hell are the niggers that ran in here" Flop doesn't say anything but he points toward the rear door that's standing open. The policeman looks at Flop with what can only be described as total disdain and hatred. "If you hide them we gone shut this shit hole down." Flop responds in a manner that most old black men have been taught. "Naw boss, they ran through here. I told them keep going. I don't want to get involved." A second policeman who entered the pool hall walks around staring into the faces of the people playing pool. He is well known because of his reputation for harassing and beating blacks. Every mother in the neighborhood warns their children to stay away from Turner. He stops in front of a man waiting to play pool." What's your name boy?" You look like one of them who ran in here. The man answers," my name is Ronnie Smith." The policeman continues his questioning. You look like a trouble maker. You just came through that door." The young man responds, "officer, I been here for at least two hours. Ronnie is saved when a call comes over the radio requesting backup and the policeman leave the pool hall but not before Turner tells Ronnie he will be back.

The pool hall scene took place out of sight of Marci and her friends but the police look in their direction as they exit and yells, "You got five minutes to get your asses off the streets." They begin to walk not knowing where to go. Marci sees Ms. Cashaw with her door open beckoning them to hurry. The girls all rush to her house and she quickly slams the door. "Stay here until it calms down, it's dangerous outside now. Call your parents and let them know you are safe." The girls call their parents and it's decided that the safest thing to do is spend the night where they are. Ms. Cashaw informs the girls that the city is under martial law and a curfew has been imposed from 6:00am to 6:00pm. Still unaware of what has taken place Marci asks Ms. Cashaw what has happened. With her head in her hands and tears flowing," Child don't you know, they killed Dr. King tonight. Somebody done shot him dead." They all have stunned looks on their faces and Kim begins to cry. Dakota consoles her even though she too is crying.

Marci is standing in the window and she notices the crowd gathering again now that the police have left. She hears noise from the corner store next door to Ms. Cashaw's house. Glass is breaking and she sees people running with food and other items. The sound of sirens again. More police along with firemen arrive. Marci notices smoke coming from the direction of the store and she realizes the store is on fire. She is tempted to go outside but she remembers the words of the policemen. Some of the men refused to leave when the police arrived. One man she knew well. Although they were not a part of the looting they were ordered to get off the streets. Most begin to comply but Red or Big Red some called him stood defiant. Red was 200 plus pounds and stood six feet and some left over. He was what some would call big boned. Several policemen surround him and attempt to cuff him but without success. Others join in and begin striking him with night sticks. One policeman is knocked to the ground and another. Blood is streaming down Red's face but the adrenalin is pumping and he seems impervious to the pain but eventually he is over whelmed and hauled away. Military trucks and armored vehicles arrive filled with National Guardmen. They exit with bayonets fixed and form a menacing line. The few people who were still loitering understood what was about to happen. They quickly left the scene.

Her curiosity was pushing her to stay in the window even after witnessing such a bloody and brutal scene but she hears gun shots and decides that being in the window is not a safe place. She joins the other girls who are lying on their pallets but wide awake. All through the night the scenario plays over and over, mobs, burning and looting, sirens, gun shots.

Months have passed and the tension is easing some but that horrible night will forever be a part of Marci's { psyche.} Sitting in the kitchen watching her mother has always fascinated her. Her mother seems to move so gracefully as if she is performing. Her mother is standing over the stove checking her pots and from there she grabs a broom and dustpan to sweep up flour from the floor and as smooth as ever she ends up in from of the old white cabinet that was given to her by her late husband as an anniversary gift. Marci ponders why her mother cherishes such a monstrosity. Marci thought she only kept it as a reminder of her husband who passed away from a heart attack several years earlier. Now it was the three musketeers, Marjorie, Rickey and Marcie. The only purpose it serves is blocking the sunlight from the window. Marci's mother always seem to find some useless trinket to put in the junk drawer. Whenever Marci questions her mother she gets the same answer as if it's the first time she is hearing the question. "Child everybody need a junk drawer. You never know when you might need some of this stuff" We throw things away never knowing how valuable they are." Marci thinks the only place for that stuff is the trash can. She recalls times that neighbors have come over looking for things and her mother would look through her junk drawer and find what they were needing or a reasonable facsimile as she called it. She recalls one particular day waking up to someone calling her mother's name. It was their neighbor Ms. Ledora or Dora for short. "Marjorie, Marjorie I'm missing a button on my dress and I can't find anything to match it in my drawer. Her mother searches her junk drawer and finds a button that is a perfect match. Marci's mind soon turns from the junk drawer and back to the fact that its summer and time for her and her crew to head to Washington Park for the first day of swimming. None of them really go to swim but Washington Park was the place to be in the summer. The boys who could afford cars pull up next to the pool and compete to see who could play the best songs. There seemed to be an unwritten rule that the first song played had to be "Summertime" by Booker T and the MG's. Marci, Janay, Dakota and Kim were on their way for opening day at Washington Park.

There is a line at Ms. Rosie's snack wagon. She had the best snowballs in town not to mention the other goodies she sold. The line was long but no one seemed to care. The atmosphere was jubilant, the sun was shining and it was opening day at Washington Park. The clock ticks down and the crowd rushes through the door with their quarters in hand to pay for fun in the sun. Soon the music battles begin. Webbie Mac pulls up in his 1956 restored power blue convertible Cadillac with white interior. He searches for his 8 track of the Temptations and selects "My Girl" On key everybody sings along. A new comer pulls up besides Webbie to challenge him. He is driving a red Dodge Charger with black stripes down the center. He calls himself Mohair because of his love of mohair coats and jackets. Someone standing nearby calls out , "Hair do something with it" Mohair pushes his Percy Sledge tape in the 8 track tape player. Soon the sound of Percy singing "When A Man Loves A Woman" creeps through the pool area. Marci screams "play my song". Some guy yells out" make it do what it do". On a few occasions females would take part in the challenge. Most of the time it was Big Sue. She drove a white on white Cadillac fresh off the showroom floor. Sue had a reputation for being not only one of the toughest women in Memphis but there were very few men willing to cross her path. After parking she finds Aretha Franklin's "Respect" Again the crowd erupts. Her future would hold both good and bad. Sue would later spend a number of years incarcerated but who would guess after being released she would make a complete turnaround in her life and write a book about her life entitled" Big Sue" At the park the competition continues as others drive up. Song after song after song. Washington Park, what a place to be. This year in particular was a bitter sweet experience. They knew this would be the last year they swam at Washington Park. Due to the racist and segregationist policies all city pools would be closing.

Marci 's thoughts switch from the park to the upcoming Fourth of July Parade. School was out but high school bands and majorettes gave up some of their summer days to practice for the parade. It was a time that brought excitement and the opportunity for the schools to show their talents. This year Manassas along with their arch rival Booker T. Washington,

Humes, and Central were chosen to participate. Manassas has a rich history and although Marci's mother only made it to the ninth grade she encourages Marci often when she speaks about the school. Manassas was established in 1899 and became the first black four year accredited high school in Shelby County. The school would later gain recognition in a documentary about the football team entitled "Undefeated". Oscar winner Issac Hayes was also a graduate of Manassas. Booker T. Washington carried a banner of it's own being the first black high school in Shelby County. Graduates from Washington included the Bar-Kays and W.W. Herenton, who was the first black mayor of Memphis's The other two schools were also noteworthy. Central High has the record for the oldest high school in Shelby County. Businessman, enterprenuer and developer Avron Fogelman and Bette Greene were graduates. The religious schoolat Temple Israel is named in honor of Fogelman and his wife as well and the southeastern leg of I-240 in Memphis is named after him. Green is most known for her Book entitled :Summer of My German Soldier which was later the title of a film. L.C. Humes was the final participant well known for the School where Elvis Presley attended and graduated in 1953. Humes occupied the same street as Manassas less than a mile apart but on the white end of the street. Marci was willing to give it everything she had to compete against Washington but even more for the opportunity to compete against Humes. Marci was willing to concede that Elvis was the king of rock but Manassas was the home of Emerson Able's "Mighty Manassas Band" and Ms. Cavenaugh's "Amazing Majorettes". Marci was 5'4", with smooth brown skin and every inch of her body was picture perfect. Kim was tall and dark with flowing black hair. This was the first year that there was a dark skinned girl on the team. The effects of racism showed itself even within the black community. It seemed that the odds were always in favor of the lighter skinned blacks. Tall and black, Kim changed that with her presence on the team and she let everyone know that she was black and beautiful. Dakota was the red bone of the group. The high yellow girl who had a hypnotizing smile. Then there was Janay, the wild one. Not quite dark and yet not bright skinned. She fell somewhere in between. She could pass for Hispanic if she spoke Spanish. Janay was the one who stood up for the others verbally and on a few occasions physically. This was the crew. Everyone knew that they were friends forever and nothing or no one could separate them.

The day arrived and Main Street was packed from end to end with festivity. Vendors lined the streets and added even more excitement with their peddler's calls "Hot dogs, hot dogs, get your juicy hot dogs. The smell of popcorn, the colorful cotton candy made it a day to remember. Marci gazed on the bright-colored floats with their messages of freedom. Marci pondered as she read some of the messages. "home of the free, land of the brave." Why was it so difficult for some to see that these words didn't apply to every American. She wrestled with the conflict inside. Why am I participating in an event that excludes me in so many ways. She feels an easing of the struggle when she realizes that there have always been people of every race who stood for justice and equality for everyone. People who gave their lives to make freedom and justice a reality for all Americans. Marci was comforted with knowing there would always be people like William Lloyd Garrison, there would always be people like the Quakers to stand up to the powers, people like Viola Liuzzo who gave the ultimate in a struggle she didn't have to join. Maybe these thoughts were something to be placed in the junk drawer to be retrieved later but they should never be thrown away.

Booker T. Washington was the second band to perform. The Central Band got a rousing reception as they performed and Washington was out to top it. Manassas was following Washington and Marci could hear the music and even see the crowd swaying to the sound. Now it was time for Manassas.

They stop at the designated place to perform. The drum major twirls his baton and the silence is teeming with anticipation. The drum major turns to the band, the band strikes up with "Watermelon Man" and Marci and the majorettes move with the rhythm that has been passed down from generations of African DNA. Marci observes the crowd and sees a crowd of young white students watching them. She assumes they are from Humes. Janay sees the group and moves closer with intent to tease. She is the bad girl and she wants Humes to know you can't touch Manassas. Their performance ends and they move on knowing that the crowd's cheers have signaled their excellent performance. Marci looks back as they continue and she locks eyes with one of the male students from Humes. They both smile briefly before she moves on. The months pass swiftly and as August arrives Marci looks forward to graduation. The closing of the public pools soon brought tragedy across the city. Several young black men drowned while swimming in the Mississippi River and area bayous. Lack of access to pools for black citizens contributes to the large number of blacks who cannot swim as well as to the drowning of some who attempt to swim in unsafe waters. Marci's brother, Rickey his best friend Jr. Bradford and two others decide to swim at the local YMCA. The closest was about three miles away and those who took the trip had to pass through Hurt Village. In the early 50's the Memphis Housing Authority built an all- white housing development in an attempt to attract whites to the area. It was named after Dr. William H. Hurt, a white doctor and philanthropist. Racial tensions are high due to Dr. King's assassination and any blacks who dare walk through Hurt village invite assault and racial slurs. Hurt Village was built for whites only and they protected it as if it were the last piece of ground on earth. No one could imagine that Hurt Village would one day be totally black and gain recognition in an award winning play as well as being mentioned in two rap songs. But for now the story was different. Rickey and his three friends are on their way through Hurt Village when they hear the familiar alarm ring out," Niggers in the village." It seems like a call for war, Whites came running from every direction and Rickey knew that was the clue to get low and go. Safe ground was South of Parkway. They were never chased pass Parkway St. Ironically Hurt Village was not the only trouble spot. Blacks who lived in other neighborhoods would sometimes assault and rob other blacks if they were not known. Rickey had faced that on more than one occasion. How could any black man be so blind not to be able to see that every black person needed each other. On the way home Rickey and his friends spotted two white youths on the edge of the black part of town. It didn't take much conversation between them to decide that they would make them pay. Rickey found a metal pipe as they got closer to the two white youths. When they were face to face he drew the pipe back. The taller of the two boys was red head and freckle faced. He froze with a look of terror on his face and immediately moved behind the smaller of the two boys. The smaller of the two boys removed his hate slowly and hung it on a fence post and very quietly looked Rickey in the face.' I'm not afraid of you because you have a pipe. With the pipe still drawn back Rickey responds in a yell" We tired of y'all messing with us." The white youth responds, "I'm sorry that you were treated like that but we had nothing to do with it." There was so much sincerity in his voice until the anger that Rickey felt melted away. He felt himself lowering the pipe and the smaller of the two boys extended his hand. Rickey reciprocated and it was a clue for the others to do the same. Everybody shook hands and went their way. The remainder of the trip home was in silence with one exception. Jr. Bradford said what they were all thinking, "Every white person is not our enemy, there are good and bad in every race. Rickey pondered on Jr's words and wondered why had he not come to that conclusion before now. Maybe he had, maybe he put those thoughts in the junk drawer to be retrieved at a later date. Rickey wondered what were the two white kids thinking.

Although the pool was closed indefinitely, Washington park was still the place to be. The music battles continued into the early fall. On one particular Saturday while Rickey and Jr. Bradford were hanging out at the park they saw a blue convertible mustang approaching. The car was not familiar and it drew everybody's attention. As the car came closer Rickey noticed the occupants were Whites. He thought to himself, surely they made a wrong turn but the driver continued. Most of the crowd mean-mugged them as they passed. To everyone's surprise the driver turned and came back toward the group of black kids and stopped. The driver and his passenger got out and headed toward Rickey. Just before he reached Rickey Moose stepped in front of him. "What you want here white boy" The driver raised his hands in submission" I ain't looking for trouble, I just came to say hello to a friend" Moose looked at him in a strange way," Friend!, you ain't got no friends here, you lost your mind. At that moment Rickey recognized the driver and his passengers as the two white kids they almost assaulted. He put his hands on Moose's shoulder, "Pump your brakes Moose I know these two, they ok". Moose stepped aside slowly with a confused look on his face like most of the other kids have and the two white kids walked up to Rickey. Rickey looks at the driver of the car," You got some balls, I tell you that. What's your name" The driver of the car extends his hand ' I'm Roy and this is Jonas, we call him Red because of his red hair and freckles. Jr. Bradford and Rickey shake hands with Roy and Jonas. Roy tells Rickey they were just riding when they saw the group of kids in the park. We never stopped before but I told Red lets take a chance and see what happens. Rickey looks back at the mustang," That's a smooth ride you got" Roy thanks Rickey and invites him and Jr Bradford to come check it out. Then Roy surprises Rickey, "Maybe we can cruise together sometime. Rickey and Jr. look at each other with the same expression and most likely with the same thoughts. Ride around in a car with two white boys. Racial tension was so high it would certainly end up in a bad way. Roy interpreted the looks on their faces and responded" I know what you thinking but we got to start somewhere.

A few weeks later Roy and Jonas show up at Rickey's house. Rickey and Jr were always together and it seemed to be the same with Roy and Jonas. Rickey's mother was standing in the door when Roy pulled up. Roy and Jonas came up and sat on the porch next to Rickey and Jr. Some of the neighbors were looking out of their windows and wondering why two white boys were at Marjorie's house. Marjorie came out and waived at her neighbors and it seemed to relive their concern. Roy and Jonas sat on the porch with Rick and Jr. Marjorie greeted the boys, "I've heard some good things about you boys. It takes courage to do what you are doing. Roy responds, "the best way to handle this is one person at a time and one situation at a time." Marci returns from the store and she immediately recognizes Roy. "You are the parade guy." Roy responds," Yea I remember you too, I didn't know Rick was your brother. Marci looks at Rick with a smile," Well I claim him sometimes." Marci's teasing brought a laugh from everyone. Roy and Marci have made eye contact again and they both seem to be spellbound until Roy realizes it and turns the conversation to Rick again." Hey guys let's take that ride. Jonas is usually quiet but he speaks up," Yea we can go through the Village and down Riverside Drive. Marci interrupts," You thinking about riding through Hurt Village with two black kids in your car. That is a recipe for trouble." Roy speaks up," I think it's a way to show people that we can respect and befriend each other. Rick added," Well you and Jonas came to the park. I guess it's time for us to reach out too. Rick's mom gives them the ok but warns them to be careful and leave immediately if there is trouble. Initially the conversation is on trivia matters as they ride along but then it turns to the racial tension that the city is dealing with. Roy opens the door to the conversation," I know there is a lot of bitterness and hatred on both sides but we don't have to feed into it. "Jr agrees with Roy, "I think about the time we met you guys. We were angry and looking for revenge but hate only begets hate. Rick asks," What can we do when it seems like the whole city is in the hate mode. Jonas adds," It starts one person at time. There are only a few of us now but who knows how many we can reach. "Jonas offers a suggestion," Maybe we can have a get together at the park." Roy turns into Hurt Village and drives slow for everyone to see that black and White kids can be friends. Some of the residents stare and others wave and say hello. Roy pulls up to a corner where several white kids are standing. Rick and Jr give each other a worried look. The car stops and Roy calls them over. "I want you to meet some of our Manassas friends." Some of the kids refused and walked away while others came to the car. One enthusiastic boy was first to reach the car," Roy who you got riding with ya." The other kids reach the car as Roy introduces them. "This is Rick and Jr." Roy introduces the four kids who came to the car. "This is Billy he is always energetic." Billy reaches over to shake Rick and Jr's hands. My name is Billy but folks call me Cannonball." The other kids take turns introducing themselves. One of the girls stepped forward and stretched out her hand, "Hi I'm Angie". Then another girl, "my name is Jo or Josephine. After she introduced herself Roy shared that he and Jo were like brother and sister. Finally the other two boys introduce themselves. Rick spoke up, "Just keeping it real I didn't think anybody in the Village was willing to hang out with us. I been chased through here a few times. Billy responded," All of us don't think that way. I have had to make haste a few times on your end of town too." Jr chimes in" What can we do when it seems like the whole city is in the hate mode." Jonas suggest a get together at Washington Park. He and Roy commit to inviting friends who are receptive and they suggest Rick and Jr do the same. Rick thinks for a minute," Well we will either have a party or a riot but we can give it a try. Rick looks at Roy," You got to get an eight track tape for your car. The park is the place for music. They all agree to reach out to as many people as possible.

Rick and Jr are a bit anxious as they walk to the park. They both are wondering how many people will show up. When they arrive at the park they count 15 people. Not as many as they would like but it was a pretty good start. Roy leads the procession of three cars from Hurt Village. The kids are waving and as they drive down Danny Thomas and they get confused looks and cold stares. One of the kids yell out," We are on our way to Washington Park. Some of the older boys see only one reason for that many whites going to the park. They come to the conclusion that it's about to go down. There is going to be a riot at the park. They send people to "Three Stories" a black housing project to let them know the whites are on their way to the park to fight. The word spreads through the project like wild fire and 20 black kids head for the park. Some of the white kids in Hurt Village have already reached the same conclusion. They only know that some of their kids are going to Washington Park and they can only be going for one reason. They round up three cars and fill them with white kids and head for Washington Park. Multiple calls have gone out to the police from residents in both Hurt Village and The Three Stories. The Police dispatcher sends the word out and calls have been made to the county sheriff and state troopers for backup. What started out as an effort to bring peace and unity has developed into a nightmare scenario. In the meantime Roy arrives with two other cars following. He has twelve people who were willing to take the risk. The two groups came together... two groups come together to greet each other. Josephine is one of the girls who decided to participate. Roy and the others remember her from their ride through Hurt Village. Rick tells Roy he is the guess so he gets first choice to play his music. Everyone is standing around in anticipation. This is the first time in park history that a white kid will be playing music in Washington Park. Roy makes his selection and the unforgettable voices of the Righteous Brothers flows through the crowd with a song that every kid white or black knows well. 'Unchained Melody" is a song that crosses all barriers and cheers go as some attempt to sing along. One of the black kids tells Jr." He hitting hard. Whoever comes next got to bring it. Webby Mac takes the challenge and chooses Gene Chandler's "The Duke of Earl". The kids have become relaxed enough to dance with each other. Rick Jr, Roy, and Jonas can hardly believe what they are seeing. The next song has to come from one of the kids that came with Roy. "Expressway to Your Heart" by the Soul Survivors is an excellent song to keep the dance party going. Roy starts looking around. Rick looks at him with a smile," looking for somebody" Roy has an embarrassed look on his face," No, no, just checking out the scene." Rick comes back, : Well the scene you looking for is walking back from the snack wagon. Roy tries to explain himself again," I wasn't looking for Marci, I was just chillin and looking around. Marci walks up to them, "hey guys it looks like everything turned out ok. She makes eye contact with Roy, "glad you came I was looking forward to seeing you." Roy looks back at Rick at a loss for words," Yea, yea, it's real good to see you too." Marci places her hand in his," Let me show you around the park." Roy's heart was racing when he first saw Marci at the parade and it seems to race even faster every time he sees her. But now that he feels her hand in his' he thinks he has to be in heaven. Marci 's brown eyes are melting Roy and he is trying all he can not to show it. Marci and Roy walk away hand in hand. Jr looks at Rick," Say I think he is a cool dude but he may be looking for a jelly roll with some brown sugar." Rick responds," I don't think so but if he is he'll find out he be messing with the wrong one. She will set him straight. Rick looks around again and thinks to himself if everyone could at least try to understand those who are different what a wonderful world we would live in. Jr. offers to show Josephine around the park. Just then he sees several cars coming in the park. He can hardly believe that more whites from Hurt Village are coming to the get together but his hopes are soon dashed when the people get out of their cars with bats, chains and other weapons. One of the white kids is leading the group, "We came to help. We got the word about the fight. The music stops and everyone begins to gather. Roy and Marci rush over," What's happening, why do you have weapons. "We came to fight." The leader of the group responded. Roy and Rick are standing shoulder to shoulder. Roy corrects him. "We didn't come for a fight. These are our friends and we are getting to know each other. Maybe it' something you need to try. The man was clearly angered by Roy's words. His face flushed, "We don't socialize with them and you know it. What's wrong with you." Rick looks up and his heart sinks when he sees a group of blacks coming with weapons. Maybe this was not a good idea after all. Maybe blacks and whites will never be able to accept each other as equals. The angry white group sees the black group coming and they face them ready to fight. Sirens are nearing and Marci thinks this is about to be a nightmare. Several cars of police, sheriffs and troopers arrive. They stop their cars in between the two groups that have squared off to fight. There are 20 law enforcement personnel present. The city police takes the lead because it is their jurisdiction. He sees three groups of people. One group of blacks and whites together and two other groups one all black and the other all white facing off with each other. Lt. Parks is a native Memphian and he is well aware of the racial tension. When he observed the groups he knew what was happening.. Lt. Parks speaks to Rick and the others and learns that the purpose of the gathering was an attempt at reconciliation. Rick and the others are surprised at Lt. Park's response. "It is an outstanding thing that you are doing. It is so very unfortunate that it is the kids who are providing the example. A few of us will remain to be sure there are no more interruptions. Lt. Parks speaks to the two opposing groups using a bull horn. "Disburse immediately unless you want a change of address." Both opposing crowds still stare at each other not wanting to be the first to back down. Lieutenant Parks gives orders to deploy tear gas. The cadre of law enforcement officers don protective masks and load gas canisters in their gas guns. This has a profound psychological effect on the crowd. Both groups begin to leave the park and some are arrested for having weapons. Marci is thinking, could it be possible that this is coming from a white police officer. Her mind travels back to the night that Dr. King was killed and what she experienced from the officers who confronted them. Roy and the others are even more surprised when a few of the group who came to fight have called up the courage to ask to join the group at the park. Marci thinks of the junk drawer. She is not the only person who has a junk drawer. There are others Black and White people who have not discarded their hopes of racial reconciliation. From time to time they have to be placed in the junk drawer for safe keeping but never thrown away. They can always be retrieved at a later date.

Time passes and graduation day arrives. Roy and Marci is a common site. Roy was being accepted as just another kid at Washington Park. Little did they know that the world of high school was about to be exchanged for one that would forever touch their lives. The horrors of war were about to invade their lives. America committed troops to the Vietnam War in 1965. The country was now three years into a war that none of the kids had heard of. Marci only recalls one of her teachers asking the class if they know where Vietnam was and what was going on in that country. None of the students knew anything about it. Like Marci they all brushed it aside. The draft was on and every male who was eighteen years old was required to register for the Selective Service Board. There were some who were too eager to reach their eighteenth birthday. They lied about their age and volunteered to join the military. Rick had a year to go before he turned eighteen. Jr. Bradford, Roy and Jonas were all draft age. The draft selections came and both Roy and Jr. Bradford were classified 1-A (Eligble for military service). Jr. Bradford didn't wait to be called but decided to join the Navy. Jonas volunteered as well but was rejected for symptomatic flat feet. Roy wanted to follow in the tradition of his father and grandfather and become a part of the Marine Corps. He knew where he was going even if he wasn't drafted. With a four point GPA Roy could easily have been given a 1-S classification for school. He decided to put school aside and be a marine.

Tonight was to be a special night for Roy and Marci. Roy had asked her out to share something with her The two of them decided to go to Berretta's at the corner of Park and Highland. It was a popular high school hangout mostly for white kids. Marci was anxious to know what Roy wanted to discuss. As they drove down Park Ave. to Berretta's, Marci felt like any other high school girl does when they are riding with that special person. She wanted the entire world to see them together. They came to a stop and Roy looked over at her and the attraction was too strong for either of them to fight it. They kiss and all the world seemed to disappear. It was only Marci and Roy. It was a world they wanted to last forever but the honking of a car horn brought them back to reality. They both smile at each other as Roy pulls away. Roy is thinking, what a wonderful night. I will always remember it. Roy pulls up to the car hop area and parks. For the second time that night Roy looks Marci in her eyes and grasps her hand, "I want this to be a special night for the two of us. I want this to be a night we can remember forever. I want to give you something to keep for me. Marci is curious, "Why am I…" Roy interrupts, "Please let me finish" I want you to keep my class ring. In my school that means two people are going steady. Marci is pleased but cautious, "It means the same thing at my school too but what about your parents." Roy eases her mind, "My father is deceased and my mother knows all about you." Marci is relieved, "I will cherish it forever. I know it's not customary for a girl to give her ring to a boy but I would like for you to keep my ring as well." They both promise to wear the rings on chains around their necks. With a serious look on his face Roy tells Marci, "There is something else I would like to tell you. I will be leaving for Marine boot camp in two days. I feel it's the right thing to do. Both my father and grandfather were marines. I want to do something for my country and honor my family tradition." Marci is stunned when she hears this. She can only recall her teacher telling her about Vietnam and all of the Americans who have died fighting. With tears flowing she hugs Roy. She tries to speak in between her sobs. "But why you? You know they will send you to Vietnam. There is so much killing." Roy holds Marci close, "I know, but anything worth keeping is worth dying for. Besides do you think I would get myself killed and not have the opportunity to spend my life with you." He pulls away from Marci's embrace and looks her in her eyes," I made a deal with death. I told death I wouldn't bother him if he didn't bother me. We shook on it." Marci looks at him with admiration as they both laugh. Roy pulls her close. Marci's warm, soft body melts into his. This time the kiss is long and passionate. When they finally separate they continue to stare into each other's eyes. Roy finally speaks, "I guess we should eat, what you think?" Marci does not respond. She lays her head on Roy's chest wishing this night could last forever. Roy feels like he can conquer the world with Marci by his side. After a while they select their meal and Roy flashes his lights for the car hop to take their order. After they eat Roy decides to drive around the city to spend as much time as possible together. They both realize it will be months before they see each other again. On their way to Marci's house, Roy pushes his eight track tape in and selects the only song to fit such an occasion. Soon the car is filled with Ben E. King's "Stand by Me" They arrive at Marci's house and there is no one outside. Roy parks and they take in all that has happened. Roy breaks the silence, "I will write you as soon as possible." Marci quickly replies," I will be waiting for them and I will respond to every letter you write. For the third time that night they kiss. Marci has never done this with anyone black or white. She slowly unbuttons her blouse and lifts her bra. She takes Roy's hand in hers and guides it to her beautiful black full breast. They kiss again and Roy is to the point of hyperventilating. They finally pull away from each other. Marci tells Roy, "I will wait forever for you to return to me." Roy is still breathing fast, "It won't take that long I promise you." Marci fixes her clothes, gets out of the car and heads to her door. She stops and looks back, Roy is still staring intently. She blows him a kiss and turns to continue down her walk. Thinking to herself, this must be how Cinderella felt. Roy pulls away feeling like he is on top of the world. Marci shares the news about Roy and her mother notices the concerned look on her face. She consoles Marci, "Baby, the same God who kept him in Memphis can keep him in Vietnam." Marjorie knows just what to say and when to say it. Marci is comforted by her mother's words. She fall asleep clutching Roy's class ring. Roy arrives home and shares with his mother about swapping class rings with Marci. Ellen responds, "It doesn't surprise me as much as you talk about her. She must be special to you. Roy's eyes light up." She is beyond special. I have never met anyone like her." Ellen is happy for Roy and Marci but she is not naïve, "I'm happy for the both of you but know that you will face an uphill battle. This is the South and it's still hard for some to accept interracial relationships." Roy confirms his mother's words, "I know there will be people of both races who disapprove. Marci and I have talked about it and we are prepared to deal with whatever comes."

Roy and Ellen begin packing for his journey to Camp Pendleton. After they finished packing he put his bus ticket on top of his luggage so it wouldn't get misplaced. Roy gets in bed but he is too hyped to sleep. His mind races as he reflects on the time he spent with Marci. He is anxious about what he will face at Camp Pendleton and eventually Vietnam. From the moment he got off the bus Roy and the other recruits experienced the shock therapy his father and grandfather told him about. The screaming, cursing and harassment is never ending. To add insult to injury, Roy watched all of his curly hair fall to the floor to the great delight of his drill instructor. The volumes of paperwork and vaccinations along with the military's hurry up and wait mentality put Roy on edge. This was more than some of the recruits could handle. Roy and the other recruits were awakened in the middle of the night by the drill instructor yelling commands. Roy would never forget the names of the men who shaped him to become a marine. Years later he would recall the names of Vasbinder, Mohome and Delasola. Vasbinder was very good at bringing what he called "scunion" down on anyone who failed to follow his commands to the letter. Roy learned later that the word meant distress, suffering and destruction. On that particular night Roy and the other recruits learned that one of their group had taken his life. Vasbinder made it a point to march each one of them to the latrine to see the blood covering the floor. The recruit had used a razor blade to cut his wrist. The training continued with day and night forced marches, sleep deprivation, hunger. The hand to hand combat was brutal and some recruits used it to settle disputes. The thirteen weeks finally came to an end and graduation was near. Roy learned that only twenty of the fifty recruits would be graduating. Some chaptered out and others were recycled to start the program over.

Roy had been in contact with Marci and his mother. He made it a point to write regardless of how tired and frustrated he was. Ellen and Marci were just as faithful in responding to his letters. Roy wanted the two special people to be present at his graduation. When Ellen received the news she drove over to Marci's house and the two of them planned their trip to Camp Pendleton. Marjorie and Ellen bonded almost immediately. Although Marci and Roy faced a challenge from those who refused to see all people as equal, they knew they had the support of their mothers. It was no surprise to Marjorie that Ellen had a junk drawer too. {They both agreed that everyone had a place where they kept items that they were not quite sure of what do with} Marjorie showed Ellen her drawer and they talked about the things they placed in their perspective drawers. The drawer was for items that stirred old memories, odd items that seemed to have no purpose but they were not willing to throw away for some reason. They realized the junk drawer was not just for trinkets. They both knew that dreams and hopes were attached to those trinkets. The junk drawer was not just for tangible items but a place that could hold their hopes and desires. A place where they could be kept and maybe one day come to fruition.

Ellen and Marci arrived on Wednesday to celebrate the two day event. On Thursday the recruits would do a final "Motivational Run" followed by time spent with their families to tour the none restricted areas. Friday was graduation day. Ellen and Marci were proud of Roy and all of the young people who persevered to become United States Marines. The marines were lined up to Pass in Review. Everyone stood proud in their Dress Blues. At the end of the ceremony Drill Instructor Vasbinder took charge of his company to dismiss them. Everyone was surprised to hear Vasbinder give the command to open ranks. This was one of the commands used to prepare recruits to do pushups. Roy thinks, surely he want make us do pushups in our Blues with our families watching. The groans and gasps flowed through the company. After a few moments of silence

Vasbinder gave the command to close ranks. Sighs of relief filled the company when they realized Vasbinder was getting his last shot at harassment. After graduation, the three of them shopped for souvenirs and had lunch. Ellen returned to the hotel to allow Roy and Marci time together. As they walked the base, Marci noticed there were several interracial couples. Marci shared with Roy that it seemed like a different world. It was rare to see so many different races married and interacting with each other. Roy agreed that military bases are safe places for interracial couples for the most part. Truman signed Executive Order 9981 in 1948 ending discrimination in the military. Although it was a huge step in the right direction, they both knew that laws cannot change hearts. Roy and Marci spent time with two grads he bonded with in basic. The three couples shared stories about their lives and how they met. Smitty was a Black kid from New York and Timothy Jones also known as "Cool Breeze" was a young White kid from Mississippi. The three of them hit it off instantaneously. The couples enjoyed each other. They laughed, joked and recalled some of the humorous moments they shared in basic. Knowing what was ahead, the conversation turned to the reality of war. All three had received orders for Vietnam and they were going to different units. It was a good possibility that they would never see each other again. It was a sobering thought but one that needed to be accepted. Tim asked a hypothetical question, "What if there were no wars? What if we could learn to settle our differences without fighting and killing each other?" There was only silence. Marci thought perhaps another dream to be placed in the junk drawer for another time. The mood was somber. Roy holds Marci and comforts her, "I'll be ok. Some things are out of our control and we have to leave them in the hands of a higher power." Marci dries her eyes before responding, "I do believe His angels will watch over you but I can't help worrying." They night ends and they all go their separate ways. Roy drops Marci off at the hotel. He tells her it will probably be two months before they see each other again. He chose to postpone his ten day leave period until he completes Infantry Training (ITB). Roy chose infantryman as his military occupation specialty(MOS). He wanted to continue in the footsteps of his father and grandfather. The nine weeks of training were grueling but he makes it through the course. With his training behind him, Roy focuses on home and spending time with Marci and his mother. When he arrives home he learns that Jr. Bradford joined the Navy and is in Vietnam. Roy makes a mental note to look him up when he gets to Vietnam. Roy, Jonas, Rickey and Cannonball pal around for a few days. He spends his last day with Marci. They cherish their time together realizing that Roy will be thousands of miles away for thirteen months. They sit silently in the old green swing on Marci's porch. Roy finally speaks, "Life changes so fast and so drastically. Sometimes we don't have time to adjust." Marci strokes his face gently before speaking, "Come back to me,, promise me." Roy senses the concern in her voice and tries to comfort her, "Nothing but God in heaven can keep me away from you." The following day Roy is off to spend thirteen months in Vietnam. He is assigned to the Third Battalion, Third Marine Regiment in Da Nang. The air field was close to the Grave Registration Unit. He witnessed the solemn looks on the faces of the men identifying and shipping the hundreds of dead service members. Soon after arriving in country, Roy's company was assigned to participate in Operation Virginia Ridge in the Quang Tri Province. Roy's unit was assigned to deny the enemy use of the area around the DMZ in the area. Roy's training prepared him for the many nights he didn't sleep, the lack of food but nothing could have prepared him for the stench of death. They surprised a company sized unit of North Vietnam soldiers. Ten were killed and two captured with only minor injuries to his unit. One of the captured soldiers was terrified. He kept his head down and shook continuously. The other captured soldier was defiant and refused to provide any information when questioned by the Vietnamese interpreter. They were both taken back to base and turned over to the intel team. Roy would later find out that John McCain was a POW at that time at the infamous Hanoi Hilton. McCain would spend five and a half years as a POW and later become one of the most well respected senators by both republicans and democrats. Roy wrote home to Marci and his mother at every opportunity. Having her ring and reading her letters helped Roy get through the tough days. This particular night was really rough on him. Marci's letters always seem to calm his spirit. Roy had read the letter twice but each time it seemed as if Marci were right by his side when he read her letter. For the third time that night he reads Marci's letter. "Hello Roy, things are going well with me. I spoke to your mother a few days ago. We talk about the letters we receive from you and how they encourage us. It's been close to nine months since I last saw you. I am praying for the remaining four months to pass quickly. I think about our night at Berretta's constantly. I keep that night in mind to keep me going until we are together again. I wish you were here with me now. I would love to feel your arms around me. I fantasize at times of you and me caressing and kissing. I would surrender to you and enjoy every moment. Marci shared that her and Josephine had become close since the day at the park and they talked often.

Roy stopped at that point because the letter also contained a sad note. Jr. Bradford's mother came by and informed them that she received word that he is MIA and has been for two weeks. When he read the news about Jr Bradford it gave him such a surreal feeling. Someone he knew and hung out with was now missing and may never be found.

He read Marci's letter again and again. He has always respected her but he too has fantasies of the two of them lying in bed together and their naked bodies pressing together. Roy knew at that point that Marci would be the girl he asks to marry him. Roy was granted two days R and R and he decided to look around the town and sample some of the local food. In town he was approached several times by young Vietnamese girls offering him sex for money. It was obvious that some were children. He managed to keep his focus and continued to one of the local eateries. Roy thinks of the terrible things that war bring. War is not just killing and mutilation but the suffering and degradation of innocent people. Roy arrived at the restaurant that was recommended and took a seat. Shortly a young Vietnamese girl came to take his order. Hello she said, my name is Binh and I'm here to take your order. {Roy was surprised that her English was very articulate.} She smiled because she saw the look of surprise on his face. She has experienced it many times working in her mother's restaurant. She explained, "My father was a soldier and he and my mother met when he came to our country. He did two tours and he spent a lot of time teaching me when I was very young. After his second tour ended we lost track of him. We don't know if he's missing, dead or just left. My mother would always have me by her side and she would ask the Americans to help me with my English. Roy felt a mixture of sorrow about her father and pride for her perseverance. He didn't quite know what to say but he knew he should say something in response to her story, "I hope you find your father someday. I know he would be very proud of you." Binh responds, "Thank you. I hope we find him but if not I will continue to live my life to the fullest. I'm not giving up. My mother taught me to put my hopes away for safe keeping but never give up on them. Roy had a week to go before his tour ended. He was assigned to one final mission before being shipped back to the states.

Roy's unit received a priority message that one of the outpost on the DMZ has not reported as scheduled. Roy was chosen to join a platoon size unit to check their status. The platoon sized unit was able to move swiftly and cover a lot of ground.

When they arrived Roy smelled a stench like never before. Roy had never smelled decaying bodies, but he knew exactly what the smell was. Their fears were confirmed when they entered the post. Three dead marines were scattered over the post and the others were missing. Flies were swarming and Roy could see maggots crawling in the wounds of the dead marines. One had a gaping hole in his head, the second marine was unrecognizable due to his face being bashed in and the third had his throat cut. Some of the men vomited and other stared in horror. One of the men screamed out in anger, "I hate gooks. I want to kill all of them." Roy felt anger as well but he restrained himself from making hateful comments. Staff Sergeant Otis Biggs was leading the unit. He was a two timer and he had seen this scenario many times before. He realized he had to get his troops focused or they would fall apart. He gave orders in such a commanding way that it shook the troops out of their surreal experience. Biggs' baritone voice could be heard all over the jungle, "What you looking at. They ain't gone say hello to you. They in marine heaven now so let's be about our business." He instructs the radioman to report the incident in order that replacements can be sent. The replacements were sent by helicopter to expedite time. Once they arrived the bodies were placed on the helicopter. There was not enough room for the entire platoon to take the chopper so Biggs decided they would all return by land. Biggs growled out orders, "Marines we did our job, lets di di mau." Roy's emotions moved from sorrow to anger, and fear. Although he felt guilty, he could not deny that his overwhelming emotion was gratitude. Although he regretted his fellow marines were dead, he was grateful that he was still alive.

Roy's tour of duty has come to an end. He makes his rounds to say farewell to some of the men he has bonded with. On his flight back to the states, Roy thinks about Jr. Bradford and prays that he will return home. With Vietnam behind him,

Roy realizes how blessed he is to live in America. He has a little less than three years of service remaining to complete his obligation. He decides to apply for OCS to become an officer once he returns to the states. For now he puts that all behind him. He thinks only of seeing his mother and Marci. Roy communicated regularly with Marci and his mother by letter and on rare occasions he spoke with them by MARS but he realized in thirteen months things may have changed. He knew his mother would always love him but was it the same with Marci. He had witnessed marines receiving Dear John letters. He had heard about others returning home and discovering that their wives and girlfriends had moved on. Roy wondered if these thirteen months had created a breach between him and Marci that could not be repaired. Ellen had written Roy and told him that the war had become very unpopular and service members were being ostracized and even physically assaulted by fellow Americans. Roy would soon get a taste first hand. Roy and some other marines wanted to visit Oceanside and they chose to wear their uniforms. Initially they received stares and a few frowns. One woman walked up to the group and called them baby killers. It was hard to imagine that they had gone through so much for a country whose government had sent them to fight and then receive this kind of treatment. They group continued on their sightseeing tour but Roy would think carefully about wearing his uniform off base from that point on.

When Roy arrived home he immediately saw some of the changes that had taken place. Black families were now a part of Hurt Village and White families had begun to move away. Roy spent the first day at home with his mother catching up on the latest news but he was anxious to see Marci. The following day he headed to Marci's house. He was greeted with a smile and a hug by Marjorie when he stepped in. Marjorie's soft voice reassured Roy that he was still in good standing with her,

"Come on in military man, so glad to have you back safe and sound." Roy hugged her tight as he responded," Thank you Miss. Marjorie, I'm glad to be home." Marjorie called out to Marci, "Marci, you got somebody here to see you." Roy didn't give Marci a definite date for his return because he wanted to surprise her. He clutched Marci's class ring as he waited. Marci came out of her room and stopped in surprise when she saw Roy. The tears began to flow as she rushed to him. They embraced and Roy's fears are wiped away. Unable to contain his emotions, tears flow from his eyes as well when he speaks, "We will never be separated again." This was Marjorie's cue that they needed some time alone. She went to her bedroom and closed the door. Marci caresses Roy's face as she speaks," I can't believe you are here. God kept you." Roy's heart rate is off the charts but he manages to get his words out, "I'm so glad I'm here with you. There were times when I felt I would never see you again. Promise me that you will always be by my side." "That's ok by me" Marci replies. Unable to control what they are feeling at the moment, they lose themselves in a heated kiss. Their hearts pound as the desire to please each other grows stronger. Roy realizes, not here, not yet. He slowly pulls away and suggests they hang out at Berretta's later that evening. Marci agrees.

They both spent the day anticipating what the evening would be like. Marci paced the floor thinking of what it would be like to spend time with Roy at their favorite spot. Marjorie saw an opportunity to tease her daughter," If you don't stop walking, we gone need to replace the floor." Marci with a look of shame responds, "Oh mama, stop it." The time passes and Roy arrives. Roy enters and greets everyone. "How are you Miss Marjorie." She tells him that she is doing well. Then he turns to Marci," and you my precious one." She answered with a bit of humor, "I'm doing fine Roy Allen Thompson and you." Roy enjoyed the playful banter with Marci and responded in kind, "Roy Allen Thompson is doing just find thank you." After a few minutes of conversation with Marjorie, the two of them left for Berretta's. Roy pulled up to the same spot they had on their initial visit to Berretta's. After parking he looks Marci in the her eyes and what he says next shocks her to her core, "Marci, I would like to have my ring back." Stunned and confused she looks at Roy as she responds, "But why? Why did you bring me here to ask for you ring. I don't understand." Roy explains, "Things have changed between us and I want my class ring back so I can replace it with this engagement ring. Marci Louise Smith, will you marry me?" Marci is without words and she finally answers, "yes, yes a thousand times I will marry you." After the proposal they order the same meal they had on their first visit to Berretta's. Roy completed the night just as he did their first night at Berretta's. Once again Ben E. King's "Stand By Me" serenaded the two as they drove home. When Marci arrived home she broke the news to Rickey and her mother. She showed them her engagement ring. After Marci settled down they broke the news to her. Rickey shared that Roy had already spoken to him and their mother about marrying you. Rickey saw a chance to tease her with his next statement, "But of course I said no way." Marjorie stops him, "you did no such thing, you acted like he wanted to marry you." Rickey hugs Marci and admits the truth, "You have my blessings. I believe you got a good man and I know he has a good woman." The three of them hug. Roy had written his mother earlier and shared his plans to marry Marci. She supported him and gave him her blessings. Rickey would be one of the groomsmen along with Cannonball and Smitty. He chose Jonas as his best man. Marci chose Janay as her maid of honor. Dakota, Kim and Josephine would be her bride's maids.

Rickey and Jo were given the task of planning for the weeding with instructions from the bride and groom. They submitted an Event Information Request for Washington Park and received approval for. Both of their parents were married in June. Roy's parents were married on June eighteenth and Marci's parents were married on June sixth. They agreed to add the dates and marry on the twenty fourth of June. Rickey and Jo had done an excellent job of decorating the area they chose. The moment arrived that everyone was waiting for. Roy and Marci had decided to write their own vows.

Roy began, "I believe heaven has put us together and only God will separate us. You are the keeper of my heart and the air that I breathe. With you by my side I can take on the whole world. Death is the only power strong enough to separate us. You never have to look far to find me because I will always be by your side. When times are good I will be by your side, when times are bad know that I will be your leaning post. I say to you Marci Louise Smith my love for you has no ending.

After Roy said his vows even some of the men are moved. Both parents are wiping tears along with some of the other women. Now they wait for Marci's response. She begins, "I can't imagine finding a person like you. If there is anyone who does not believe in miracles, I say to you we are living proof. Whatever challenges we face know this, I will be by your side and we will overcome them together. The love I have for you will only grow stronger with time. I say to you Roy Allen Thompson, my love for you has no ending. The ceremony ends and Roy kisses his bride. Washington Park has reached a new milestone. Washington Park would not only be remembered as a wonderful place to enjoy but now it will be known as the place where dreams come true. They both knew that dreams deferred were not dreams lost. Marci's dreams of racial reconciliation , Roy's dreams of a world without wars, Binh's dream of finding her father only needed to be kept in the junk drawer for safekeeping.

TOGETHER AGAIN

Dokata stares into the clouds as the plane approaches Memphis. Although it has been fifty-seven years since graduating from Manassas High School and the death of Dr. King, the events are so vivid in her mind. She sees the fear and confusion on the faces of her friends. Marci's, Janay's and Kim's faces are forever carved in her conscious. She realizes they saw the same thing on her face. The burning and looting is still vivid in her mind. The helpless look on Joey's face when he was pleading with the men to stop destroying his store. Her thoughts shift to her previous trips to Memphis and the ride they can't resist taking through the old neighborhood. Thomas Street Liquor Store has long passed off the scene. The abandoned building reflects the years of neglect, but the events of that night can never be erased by any amount of time. An overgrowth of trees and weeds now replace the houses that were once familiar scenes. She remembers Mrs. Cashaw motioning to them to hurry to her house. Every year she makes the trip the scenes play in her head as if it were happening again. Janay and Marci stayed in Memphis but Kim had a wondering spirit like her and decided to move to DC. She always looked forward to seeing her road dogs again when they all played catch up on their lives. They talked from time to time but it was never enough time for all of the details.

The old Manassas was replaced by a new modern building. She realized that it was good to have the new school but her memories were of the times she and her crew walked through the halls of the old school. She reflected on the teachers who were her favorites and those who were not so favorite. She remembers the boys who walked the halls and asked to carry her books for her. The names of her class members who had passed away started flooding her mind and she felt the sadness creeping in. Some died in pursuit of fast money and fame. She remembered Mitchell who had been stabbed several times and his body placed in a barrel. Alex who was found hanging in his mother's kitchen. Cynthia was found shot to death in her living room. No one ever found out who committed these crimes. They lived the high life, and it was highly suspected that they stole drugs from the wrong people and paid the price. There were also classmates who did well in life. She remembers Issac Hayes who became known worldwide with his Shaft album. James Govan was another who became a local attraction on the famous Beale Street. To the surprise of many, some became preachers/pastors and business owners. Most of her classmates were just average people who took on life and its challenges with their heads held high. She was looking forward to meeting with her friends and catching up on the news both good and bad.

The years have brought about some changes. Dr. King's birthday was made a federal holiday in 1983 when President Reagan signed the bill into law. By 2000, every state had made the day a state holiday. It was a long hard fight, but it finally came to fruition. The bill was introduced just four days after Dr. King's assassination by Congressman John Conyers; however, it was not until 1979 that (HR 5461) was able to reach the house floor for a vote. President Carter expressed his support for he bill but it was not enough. The years passed with other attempts and failures. Those who opposed the bill wanted to water it down by removing Dr. king from the bill and renaming it by another name. With persistency, the fight was continued and President Reagan finally signed the bill on November 2, 1983. A hard-fought battle, but one that was well worth it. The city and county has had black mayors since the sixties along with black police chiefs and county sheriffs. These were indeed exceptional achievements, but none inspire her more than the two-time election of a Black man as President of the United States. Barack Obama won back-to-back elections in 2008 and 2012 against two white male republicans. Dakota's mind reflects on McFadden and Whitehead's song 'Ain't No Stopping Us Now'. She felt like the country had finally turned the corner on systemic racism and America had finally listened to Dr. King's words "Judge a man by the content of his character and not by the color of his skin".

WHERE TO NOW

But now in 2025, she feels as if the times have been reversed. On January 6, 2021, the U.S. Capital was attacked in an attempt to stop certification of electoral votes for the 2020 presidential election. One police died from a stroke a day after the attack, in addition four other officers died by suicide within seven months. 174 police officers were injured as result of the attempted overthrow.. Impeachment proceedings were brought against Donald Trump for inciting the insurrection which were subsequetly stopped by the republican majority in the Senate. The total cost of the attempted overthrow to the tax payers was $2.7 billion dollars. After Trump was placed in the White House in 2024, he granted clemency to nearly 1,600 people connected to the January 6 insurrection. Still trying to rap her head around such unbelievable events, Dakota again reflected on Marci's story about her mom's junk drawer. Marci's mom would always say 'Everyone needs a junk drawer, never throw anything away. Put it in the junk drawer and you can always go back to get it'.

It seems as if the country has abandoned the words freedom and justice for all. It seems as if those words are only meant for a few. After Obama's election, she thought the country would never turn back to the dark days of hatred but now she can only open her junk drawer and place her hopes and dreams back inside. They will remain safe until such a time that they can be taken out and enjoyed again. As devastating as the times are, she promised herself she will never throw her hopes away but keep them safe until she can once again remove them from her junk drawer and continue to pursue them.

Marci is on high alert waiting for her friend to land at the airport. Her twins, Roy Jr. and Mattie have both graduated from college and are pursuing their careers. Roy Jr. followed in his father's footsteps and chose the military. He retired from the U.S. Army with the rank of colonel. He continued his love for his country and the military by becoming an instructor for the JROTC program at Manassas High School. He too like his father did one combat tour. He carries with him the faces of the Iraqi kids who ran behind his convoy and the gunner throwing candy out and watching the kids faces shine as they scrambled for it. He laughs when he remembers the day his unit ran across their first camel spider. An entire platoon of soldiers with M-16's faced one camel spider, but they all scattered in fear. U.S. Army zero, camel spider, one. He thought it was good that the Iraqis didn't enlist camel spiders. He remembers the rockets shaking his quarters as he and his fellow soldiers relaxed on their down time. He remembers talking with the detainees at the detention center. He was amazed to discover that some spoke perfect English and they had so many things in common. He could never forget the riots that occurred from time to time. The compounds burning. The shouting and the cursing, the fires that seemed to reach the clouds when the detainees burned their housing areas. All of these things he would carry with him until his dying day but what he held on to most was the talks he had with some of the detainees. They were men with families who shared their hopes and dreams. Men who one day hoped to be released and return home to continue their lives.

Why is it that all humanity can't live together in peace. Is it the grand scheme of some to create chaos and confusion, to spread fear and hatred, to divide us for their own selfish and greedy ends?

Marci too looks forward to their ceremonial ride through the North Memphis area they grew up in. Through the grace of God and persistence the crew as they call themselves have had the opportunity to visit many places around the world but they will forever hold 'Scutterfield' as home. How the neighborhood got the name is not clear. It is rumored that it was named after a prominent businessman. Regardless of how it came about, the crew will always love Scutterfied aka 'The field' Marci'sr mother has passed away but she feels that her mother knows she has fulfilled her dreams of moving out of Scutterfield, buying a home and raising a family. Although she is not present to see it, Marci believes with all of her heart that her mother knows that Marci kept her dreams safe in the junk drawer where nothing or no one could take them from her and now they have come to fruition. Her mother's words reminds her of a quote by William James, "Your hopes, dreams and aspirations are legitimate. They are trying to take you airborne, above the clouds and above the storms, if you let them."

Mattie is an amazing person. Her open personality makes her well suited for her career as a cruise ship hostess. She loves socializing with the guests and creating a warm and friendly atmosphere. Carnival Cruise Line is the perfect place for her to meet people and listen to their life stories. She recalls an occasion when she met an elderly white lady from Mississippi who brought back memories of her mother's stories. The lady was widowed and living alone so she decided to do something she had never done before. One of her friends suggested she take a cruise so off she went. During the conversation Maggie Mae, as she wished to be called, shared a story about her childhood. They were poor and her parents didn't have a lot. She remembers her mother telling her that every penny must count. Maggie Mae painted a vivid picture of the old dresser that her mother had in her bedroom. She remembers her mother, father and herself placing all sorts of things in the drawer. When she was young she often wondered why they kept such a monstrosity and why for God's sake did they put all of that junk in that one particular drawer. Her mother told her that was the ' keep it drawer". From that point on whenever she was tempted to throw anything away she would run it by her parents and they would let her know it was ok to throw it away or they would say ' That should go in 'The Drawer'. Some things were never meant to be thrown away no matter how old and useless they may have seemed to be. She recalled her bike needed repairing one day and her father rummaging through the drawer to find a part. Much to her surprise he found a substitute for the part and was able to fix her bike. Just before bed she would sit around and listen to her parents. They would often speak of the hard times and struggles they were having but without fail one of them would say 'That one is for The Drawer, we won't give up on that dream'. So for Maggie 'The Drawer' became a symbolic place for her to place all of her unfulfilled hopes and dreams.

Mattie was in awe as she listened to the story. She thought to herself,' Is it possible that everyone has a place to store their dreams and hopes, is it possible that everyone has a junk drawer. Mattie realized that age, race, gender, and economic status were outward differences. She realized that we all have unfulfilled hopes and dreams that we refuse to let go. She decided then that she would do everything within her power to make this one of Maggie Mae's best memories. She divided her time among the guest, but she always found time to spend with Maggie. There was a connection that drew them closer and closer. They agreed to exchange numbers and stay in touch with each other. Maggie thanked her at the end of the cruise and let her know that she had made this one of her best experiences ever. As she waved Maggie good-bye it occurred to her that perhaps helping others live their dreams may be the key to seeing hers come to fruition. She pondered, there are probably some who have lost all hope of achieving their dreams. There is no junk drawer for them to store their dreams. Maybe, just maybe there is room in my junk drawer to store the hopes and dreams of those who do not have a junk drawer. Mattie thought to herself, I can be like a pacer in a 100-mile race. I can run along beside the person pursuing their dream and encourage and support them until they reach the finish line. Only it's not a physical race but a race to achieve their dreams. It's encouraging when you see others reaching their goals. It gives you the motivation to keep trying to achieve your own goals. When you help others to achieve greatness it inspires you to strive for greatness as well. Mattie is reminded of one of Dr. Martin Luther King's quotes, "Life's most persistent and urgent question is, What are you doing for others?" Mattie decided from that day forward to make room in her junk drawer for the dreams of others.

Kim's flight has landed at the Memphis International Airport and she is waiting on Dakota, Janay and Marci to pick her up. She sits impatiently, partially looking at Facebook on her phone and looking around for her crew. She is caught off guard when Dokota slips behind her and places her hands over her eyes. She lets out a squill knowing that it is one of her crew. She jumps up and they all hug and a few tears fall. Back together again.

Although it has only been a year they hold each other as if it has been forever. Dakota or Kota as she is now called walks with Kim as they both pull their luggage they play catch up. Time has brought about a change in them physically, but they still laugh and point and giggle like schoolgirls when they get together. Time will never diminish the friendship they have among each other. They all laugh and talk, but soon the crew will learn that one of them is coming to the end of the journey. For now, she keeps it to herself. There will be time to share the news later.

Once they get settled in the crew heads out for their ceremonial ride through Scutterfield. Dakota and Kim ride up front, Janay and Marci are riding in the back. They ride through the neighborhood remembering people and events but after a while Janay is quiet. They ride a little further and Marci notices Janay has turned her head toward the window and she begins to sob. Marci asks "what's wrong , why are you crying." Dakota and Kim hear the conversation and ask Marci what's wrong. Dakota pulls over and Janay can no longer hold back her tears. She begins to cry uncontrollably as she falls in Marci's arms. Kim teases Janay. "Big cry baby stop it, we feel a little nostalgic too, but don't you think you are over doing it." Janay raises up," This will probably be my last ride with you. My doctor has given me two to six months to live. I have metastatic breast cancer." Everyone is silent. No one knows what to say. Soon the tears flowed again but this time they all cry. It was devastating news to learn that one of the crew members would soon be gone. The ride through Scutterfiled holds a special meaning knowing that this will probably be Janay's last ride with the crew. After a while the tears stop but no one spoke. Janay breaks the silence,"Say mannnn ya got a pennnny" Laughter now replaces tears. They all look at Janay and yell together "Penny Man." Penny Man was the elderly gentleman who stood in front of the neighborhood store asking people for pennies. He said it in a way that caught everyone's attention. He put emphasis on the words man and penny in such a way that you could never forget it. The fact that he only asked for a penny and the strange way he asked earned him much more than the penny he asked for. Janay is smiling now and so are the other crew members. Looking in the faces of her forever friends she speaks, "He made my day when he asked for the penny. He called everyone man regardless of their gender, but no one got offended. I just thought about him. Look around, we are on the lot where the store was, and it made me think about him. The store is no longer here, but Penny Man will be remembered forever.

The crew is aware now and Janay will have the support of her besties to help her in her fight. They vow to do whatever is necessary to keep her happy and comfortable. They decide they will all sleep over at Janay's place. They move furniture around to make room for blankets to lay on the floor just as they did in high school. Popcorn and sodas are passed around and they talk into early morning. On the following day Kim and Dakota contact their families and employers to make arrangements for an extended stay in Memphis. After breakfast they settle down to talk more. Kim asks Janay what she would like to do. Janay replies, "I remember Marci's mother talking about her junk drawer. Marci too would talk about it when it seemed like things weren't going well and we wanted to give up. Eventually we all understood the potential of having a junk drawer for our dreams. My dream of a career in law enforcement came to fruition and now that I am retired, I want to do something to help others realize their dreams. Do you think it's possible for us to do this?" I would like to take the junk drawer to places where people have long given up on their dreams to help them realize their dreams do not have to be abandoned. I know we can't make everyone's dreams come true, but we can help some even if it's just one person. So what do you think?" Marci agrees, "We can't travel long distances because of our resources and Janay's health, but there are enough people in the tri-state area to reach out to." Kim gets onboard. "Yea there are plenty of people in Tennessee, Mississippi and Arkansas who could use some help and encouragement." Dakota makes a suggestion, "Maybe we can call it the Drawer of Dreams." For the time being Janay's health issue is set aside while the crew begins planning for their endeavor. One of the crew suggested having someone make a light weight drawer small enough to carry. Someone else comes up with the idea of putting motivational quotes in the drawer. It would not only be a place where dreams are kept but a place where people could receive encouragement as well. They all looked up quotes and began sharing them.

In her search Dakota ran across a quote from Arthur Ashe, who was the first Black tennis player to achieve worldwide recognition. "What do you think about this one from Arthur Ashe?" 'Start where you are. Use what you have. Do what you can.' Kim shares one from digital artist Michael John Bobak. "All progress takes place outside the comfort zone." It's now Janay's turn. She chose a quote from artist Pablo Picasso. "Only put off until tomorrow what you are willing to die left undone" Marci chooses a quote from Mike Gafka Senior WW Business Strategy Manager for Hewlett Packard. "To be successful, you must accept all challenges that come your way. You can't just accept the ones you like." Dokata shares another quote. This one is by Thomas Edison, "Many of life's failures are people who did not realize how close they were to success when they gave up." Kim chooses one by James Dean an American actor, "Dream as if you'll live forever, live as if you'll die today." Dakota chose a quote from Beyonce Knowles," The most alluring thing a woman can have is confidence." Janay asked, "What about this quote from Dolly Parton" 'If you don't like the road you're walking , start paving another one.' Marci reads a quote from Michael Jordan, "I've missed more than 9000 shots in my career. I've lost almost 300 games. 26 times, I've been trusted to take the game winning shot and missed. I've failed over and over and over again in my life. And that is why I succeed." They continue on their quest to find quotes for the junk drawer aka dream drawer. Once they fill the drawer with quotes they decide that each of them will find one person each to help make their dreams come true. Kim recalls a recent news story about a twelve year old girl in Olive Branch who has a dream of becoming a country western singer. The news crew filmed Randi singing Dolly Parton's I will Always Love You. Randi's parents don't have the money to hire a voice coach. They were hoping talent scouts were watching her performance. Kim decided she wanted to be Randi's dream partner. After contacting the news station and giving her information she asked that they give it to the McGuire family in hopes that they would meet with them. A few days passed and she received a call from a gentleman with a deep southern accent. 'Hello, this is Randy McGuire, can I speak with Kim?' Kim was excited to hear from the family and they set a date and time to meet.

The crew pulled up to the McGuire home feeling a little anxious. This was their first attempt, and they were hoping everything went well. They were met by a slightly over-weight white female who introduced herself as Rose. Randi and her father Randy were sitting at the kitchen table as they rounded the corner. He stood and invited them to sit in his deep Southern drawl. Randi was quiet and smiling, which automatically drew a smile from each of the crew. Once they were all seated Kim began to explain why they had decided to help their daughter. We grew up in a time when our parents placed things in what we called a junk drawer. Marci's mother was the person who inspired us to expand the junk drawer to include not only material things but our dreams as well. The things placed in the junk drawer were kept for such a time as they were needed. The same holds true for our dreams. We should never abandon them, but they should be put away in a safe place until the time arises to pursue them. Rose comments, "Well honey, I think everybody has a junk drawer. We got one too and its stuffed full of all kinds of things." Randy has a curious look on his face as he speaks," I just want to know why you want to help us. I mean I appreciate it but why us?" The words that Kim speak makes it clear why they were there," Dreams are color blind. The color of a person's skin doesn't keep them from dreaming. They know no economic barriers. Dreams are for the rich and the poor. Dreams are not concerned about your gender. Dreams are for everyone. We are here to help Randi follow her dreams. We have come to the conclusion that our dreams may be connected in some way. If we help someone archive their dreams it's just possible that it will lead to them helping someone else achieve theirs." Kim informed the family that Sun Studio is waiting on a call to set up an audition for Randi. Randy was overwhelmed with gratitude and Rose could not hold back her tears. Janay passes the junk drawer to Kim and she tells the McGuire family to put their dream in writing and place it in the drawer. Once it is completed, Kim leaves the family with a parting word of encouragement. "Remember, never give up on Randi's dream. It will be safe in the junk drawer."

After a few days of searching, Janay chooses her dream partner. Janay's friend Cassie works at a local assisted living facility. She told Janay about a ninety-five-year-old man who has a dream of flying in an airplane. At ninety-five Horrace Higginbotom's health and sense of humor are in good condition. Horrace has been given the nick name Joker. He loves telling the new employees the underwear joke. When he spots new employees, he makes his move. "Excuse me, do you know what type of underwear seniors like most?" The employees are caught off guard and their usual response is 'I don't know' Horrace's face lights up when he hears that and he gives them his tagline. "Well, it depends" Horrace has told the joke a hundred times, but he laughs as if it's his first. Horrace's laughter entertains them more than the joke does.

Horrace's second favorite is his denture joke. On one particular day a man was visiting Horrace's roommate. Horrace walks over to the man, greets him and before he gets a response he asks, "How is the moon like dentures" The man looks surprised which is Horrace's cue to respond, "they both come our at night." The man gives Horrace a smile mostly because his day has been brightened to see one of the residents so full of life. Horrace has never had the opportunity to fly on a plane. He looks up often when he sees one flying over. Almost everyone, staff and residents have heard him say, "Um gone ride you one day before I die" Janay wonders why Horrace has never had the opportunity to fly because it is such a common occurrence but pushing that aside she and her dream crew set out to make his dream come true. Janay has already been given permission from the administrator to visit with Horrace. The dream crew is seated in the conference room when Horrace strolls in. Horrace is unaware of the visit, and he hesitates when he enters the room. Janay speaks," Hello Mr. Higginbotom, I understand you are quite the jokester around these parts." Horrace relaxes after hearing this and he sees the opportunity to get one in. "Hello ladies, can you tell me how husbands are like lawn mowers?" Marci responds, "No Mr. Higginbottom, we don't know" Delight crosses Horrace's face. "Well I'll tell ya. They are hard to get started, they give off bad odors and they don't work half the time." Horrace starts laughing before any of the crew. They all laugh just simply absorbing some of Horrace's energy. His laughter and energy is contagious. Feeling relaxed now, Horrace sits believing the strangers are new staff members. Marci asks Horrace, "what is one of the things on your bucket list" Horrace again unaware that his dream of flying is closer than he thinks. "Fly through the sky like a bird. I never been on an airplane, maybe it will happen one day before I die." Janay sees her opportunity," Mr. Higginbottom" Horrace interrupts. "Mr. Higginbottom was my daddy, call me Horrace." Janay continues, "Ok Horrace. We are the dream crew. We seek out people to partner with to help make their dreams come true. With a suspicious look, Horrace replies, "Is that so?" Janay begins to cough uncontrollably and she steps out of the room with Marci following. Horrace looks at her with concern," Take care yourself honey. Maybe you need to see a doctor. Kim gets Horrace's attention. "Thank you Horrace, but you can believe we will take good care of her and see that she gets whatever she needs." Janay is the reason we are here. She chose to partner with you to help make your dream of flying become a reality.

We have scheduled a flight for you to Nashville and back with the opportunity to dine at the restaurant of your choice in Nashville."

After a pause Horrace speaks," I really didn't think it would ever happen. All my folks are gone and I ain't got a lot of money. I just kept the dream alive by looking up when I saw a plane passing over and thinking about what it would be like to be riding on it." Janay and Marci come back in the room. Horrace looks at her intently, "You a special kind of person. You and the others. Thank you for helping an old man see his dream come true. Thanks to every one of you." Janay tells Horrace to write his dream on paper, and she passes the dream box to him. "Put your dream in the junk drawer/dream drawer. It will be safe until it comes to fruition. Once again Horrace thanks them but he can't pass on the opportunity to tell a parting joke. "Say before you leave ladies I like to ask you a question. Where can a single man my age find a young woman who is interested in him?" Janay answered, "Well Horrace that's a tough one." Horrace replies, "You can go to the bookstore and look in the fiction department." The crew leaves with Horrace's reverberating laughter ringing in their ears.

The crew said very little about Janay's coughing while they were visiting Horrace, but they surrounded Janay and expressed their concern when they reached the car. She appeared weak as she looked into the faces of her forever friends. Nevertheless, she attempted to reassure them. "I'm ok. Some days are better than others, but I'm going to be ok." Instinctively, they know it's time for a group hug.

Marci's mind reflects on Roy and his experience in Vietnam. She remembers Roy's conversation with Binh, the Vietnamese waitress. She begins to relive the sadness when she read Roy's letter about Binh's desperate search to find her American father. She pictures the abandoned children left by American soldiers when the war ended. Because of the fear of being imprisoned or executed, many of the Vietnamese women abandoned their children they conceived by American soldiers. These children were left to the streets to fend for themselves. The children's plight was aptly stated in the name they were given, 'Children of the Dust'. Marci had decided to be a dream partner with one of the Vietnamese people who were trying to immigrate to America to find their father. Marci found several resources to help her in her quest. The Guardian US was a good source to begin with. It is an online paper that addresses the Amerasians who desire to immigrate to America. She read about the Amerasian Homecoming Act that gives assistance to Amerasians desiring to come to America. There were other organizations as well. The Amerasian Child Find Network and Amerasians Without Borders. Marci contacted The American Embassy and Consulate in Vietnam and she was given the contact information for Duong Pham. Pham is a fifty year old Amerasian whose visa has been denied. Although it has only been one month since contacting Duong, the two of them have grown close. Duong's visa was denied due to insufficient documentation. He shared with Marci that he is not sure about his father's location or if the name he has is correct. He believes that his father lives somewhere in Arkansas. Marci shared Roy's story about meeting Binh and how that stirred her to reach out to become his dream partner. Duong believes his father is a Caucasian male named John Robert Shaw and he is somewhere in Arkansas. Marci told Duong about the junk drawer slash dream drawer. She asked Duong to tell her about his dream of coming to America and meeting his father. Marci wrote his words down and put them in the junk drawer for safe keeping. She explained that the junk drawer was a symbolic place to keep dreams safe while they are pursued. The purpose of the junk drawer was to allow dreamers to reflect on their dreams from time to time and never lose hope.

Marci got busy and was able to locate a John Robert Shaw in Proctor Arkansas with the help of Spokeo. Marci called the number she was given and spoke to an elderly gentleman who answered to the name she was searching for. After a few minutes of polite conversation Marci told John her reason for calling. He explained that he nor his two sons had ever been to Vietnam. Hearing this Marci felt disappointment creeping in, but John gave her hope when he informed her that he has a first cousin named John Hershel Shaw who fought in the Vietnam war. He further stated that he moved to California a few years back. John agreed to call his cousin and see if it was ok to give his phone number to Marci. Marci wrote Duong to inform him of her findings while she waited on a response from the Shaw family. Duong wrote back to Marci," I was hoping that this was the last time I would be disappointed, but I am not loosing hope as long as there are people like you in the world and as long as my dream is safe in the junk drawer." Marci agreed to continue searching until all avenues were exhausted.

Janay can no longer ride with the crew. Her illness has caused her to slow down drastically. The pain and other issues caused by her illness has confined her to her bed. Janay's family sits with her around the clock. The hospice nurse has informed the family that she is nearing the end of life. She requested her crew to come by sensing that this is most likely the last time they will all be together. Marci, Dakota, and Kim gather around her bed. Janay can only speak in whispers. She tells them she is waiting for one more person. They wonder who else could Janay be waiting for, her family is present, and her crew is present. They soon find out when Cassie walks through the door. Cassie and Janay met at a city conference focused on pooling resources to help the homeless and elderly. While working as a police officer, Janay discovered that many of the homeless and elderly ended up in jail due to lack of resources and family support. At one of the conferences Janay and Cassie were sitting next to each other and began a conversation. They were both surprised to discover that Cassie was an alum and a cheer leader from Humes High School. Although Cassie was White and grew up in a different setting, the two of them discovered that they had a lot in common. They both loved cheering and they both had a passion to help others. The crew remember Janay talking about Cassie, but they had no idea they were that close. Janay struggled to sit up in bed. She beckoned for her crew to come closer along with Cassie. Janay then asked that Cassie be her replacement in the dream crew. They all agreed. Janay felt like she had carried her baton as long as she could and she was happy to know that she would have someone just as committed as her to carry on. It was very difficult to see Janay the way she was. They recalled the fourth of July parade in their senior year. They remembered how Janay teased the Humes High students, because she was 'The bad girl.' After a few more minutes of visiting, they decided to end the visit and allow Janay to rest. Each of her crew members gave Janay a long hug knowing that it would be her last.

Cassie is now a member of the dream crew. She has an idea of what to expect from her conversations with Janay. She realizes most of all that having a heart to help others see their dreams come true, qualifies her to be a member of the dream crew. It doesn't take Cassie long to find her dream partner. Michael Tiller is a distant relative of the well-known Tiller family Everybody in Memphis, Mississippi and Arkansas knew of the Tillers. Very few, Black or White , dared to make enemies of the Tillers. To some they were notorious gangsters but to others they were good people and even heroes from time to time. Stories have circulated about the Tiller's saving correctional officers and other inmates from death and or sexual assaults. They lived hard and some died hard, but Cassie had seen enough of Michael Tiller's life to know that he deserved a chance at fulfilling his dream of going to college. Michael dropped out of school in the tenth grade and began working to help his mother with his two siblings. The jobs he could get were low paying with long hours, but he worked them long enough to see his two siblings graduate from High School. After his mother passed, Michael resigned himself to the life he now lived, but not without occasional dreams of attending college. Cassie met Michael through his father who was one of her classmates before he dropped out of school. She took an interest in him and contacted him from time to time. Over the years she saw that there was something good in Michael regardless of what his last name was. Cassie recognized that there was racial disparity especially in the South, but she also recognized that there was also disparity toward poor Whites. She had heard the word "nigger" more times than she could imagine, but she also heard the demeaning words used to describe poor Whites as well. "Poor white trash," 'cracker", "peckerwood," "clay eater." Different words target different people, but with the same purpose. Too many of the people who are in power care little for those who are powerless, Black or White. Cassie reached out to Michael who was now 55 years old. She told him of her plans to help him achieve his dream if he were willing to see it through. Cassie agreed to help Michael prepare. The first step was to accompany Michael to the library and help him get online to take the GED Practice Test. After he receives a passing score on the GED Ready practice test she plans to have him scheduled for the actual test within the sixty-day time period. The last step is to have Michael submit his application to the college of his choice along with his GED diploma and official transcript. Michael was eager and Cassie was willing to see it through. Cassie told Michael about her newfound friends and her acceptance as a member of the dream crew. Michael wrote his dream down and met with the crew who passed him the junk drawer to place his dream in for safe keeping.

A Parting Of Friends

It was early on a warm Saturday morning. Marci and Roy were drinking coffee and enjoying time together. The phone rang. Roy answered and listened for a short period, before passing the phone to Marci without speaking. There was no need for words, Marci read Roy's expression accurately, The bad girl of the crew had teased for the last time. Janay's family informed Marci that she had made a quiet and peaceful departure. Marci took the task of calling the other crew members to inform them. It seemed that they all knew what the call was about even before the words were spoken. The following week Janay was laid to rest. Her family was well aware of the close ties she had with the dream crew members. They had requested that the hearse take the ceremonial ride that they did each time they came together. The driver began at the site of the old Manassas High School to Danny Thomas Blvd. The crew thought about the Harlem House Restaurant that was long since torn down. The time they spent eating the famous hot dog specials after games. They continued on Danny Thomas toward Marble Street. Danny Thomas and Marble would be forever carved in their heads. It was there that they saw angry men destroying The Thomas St. Liquor Store. Joey's pleas will never be forgotten. It was the same corner that made the Penny Man famous. The same place that brought back fear and disappointment each time they drove by and yet there was still a place for hope. The ride continued a little further to Chelsea and Danny Thomas. They remembered so well that this was one of the dividing lines between the Black and White parts of North Memphis. At one time, Hurt Village, the all-white housing project, was just a few blocks from this intersection. It has been demolished and replaced. New housing now occupies the area with a new name," Uptown." So many changes have taken place, some positive and others, well, only time will tell. Cassie, Dokota, Marci, and Kim stand at the gravesite listening to the familiar words spoken at so many burials. "Earth to earth, ashes to ashes, dust to dust."

THE SHOW MUST GO ON

Weeks have passed since Janay's funeral. The crew has been in contact with each other, but Dakota, who is the last to find a dream partner, has not shared anything with the others. She realizes that Janay's loss has dampened their spirits too long. She comes to the conclusion that the best way to honor her is to continue their efforts to help fulfill dreams for those who may have loss hope. She soon finds a potential dream partner. Lonnie comes to mind. Lonnie is the gentleman who takes care of her lawn. He has expressed the desire to purchase his first home; however, he has had some setbacks. She gives him a call and asks if she can partner with him to help him achieve his dream of home ownership and he agrees. Lonnie explains that he feels overwhelmed whenever he thinks about buying a home. He realizes there are so many things that can go wrong. Dokota agrees to help him do some research to help ease the stress. She puts her methodical mind to work and gathers the necessary information for Lonnie. They agree to discuss the issue when he comes over to do her lawn. She gathers thirteen key aspects that should be considered. Lonnie is becoming overwhelmed again because there is so much to consider. He thumbs through the list. 1. Get pre-approved,2. Speak to more than one lender//3. Do research on your realtor/4. Never waive the home inspection and choose a compotent inspector/ 5. Do not committ to a payment beyond your resources,/6. Overlooking the neighborhood/ 7. Good real estate atty/ 8. Research loan types 9. /Up front cost/ 10, do not use up entire savings//11. Don't drag your feet or make hasty decisions/12. Realiatic about renovation cost/13. Keep an open mind.

Dakota notices Lonnie's frustration. She encourages him." I realize it's frustrating the first time around, but think about it, You will be the first in your family to own a home and you can give them the support they need to follow your example. Lonnie shakes his head in agreement and vows to stay with the process until he is a new homeowner. The dream crew gathers around Lonnie and they pass him the junk drawer and watch him place his dream of home ownership in the drawer. He says with enthusiasm," It will be safe there until I move into my new home." They gather around Lonnie to congratulate him before he leaves.

Each of the dream crew members have partnered with someone to help them with their dreams. Some of the dreams have already come to fruition while others are still in the making. Come what may, the crew is pleased that they have made the effort to help others make their dreams come true. They accept that time will eventually bring them to a point where they can no longer partner up with other dreamers. They know that time brings an end to life, but it can never bring an end to dreamers, and it can never bring an end to the junk drawer. They decide to look for suitable replacements for the next generation of dream partners.